Noah Chases the Wind

For Noah, and for all children who can see the colors of the wind
—Michelle Worthington

For all those who taught me to see the world differently
—Joseph Cowman

Published by Redleaf Lane
An imprint of Redleaf Press
10 Yorkton Court
Saint Paul, MN 55117
www.RedleafLane.org

First edition 2015
Book jacket and interior design by Jim Handrigan
Main body text set in Ainslie
Typeface designed by insignie

Manufactured in Canada
21 20 19 18 17 16 15 14   1 2 3 4 5 6 7 8

Library of Congress Control Number: 2014938462

Noah Chases the Wind

Written by
Michelle Worthington

Illustrated by
Joseph Cowman

Redleaf Lane

Noah knew he was different.

He could see things that others couldn't,
like the patterns in the dust that floated
down on sunbeams.

He could smell the green tang
of the ants in the grass.

He could feel when a big storm was coming before the leaves on the trees even started to tremble.

Noah liked to find out how things worked,
where they came from, and where they went.

When he couldn't understand,
it hurt his head and his heart.

His room was overflowing with books of every shape and size on every subject he could imagine. Noah loved books more than he loved toys.

His favorite books were about science, especially the weather. They taught him why rain clouds looked so angry, why the air buzzed before lightning struck, and why his skin turned darker in the summer sun.

Yet search as he might, none of his books could tell him what he really wanted to know.

Noah knew where the wind came from—
but where did the wind go?

His mother was usually more helpful than his books, but she didn't know either.

"Why don't you try finding the answer for yourself?" she said.

Noah sat quietly with his back to the
trunk of his biggest tree and waited
for the wind to come.

Before the leaves on the trees even started to tremble,
Noah felt a stirring deep inside. He stood, his face to the sky,
and felt the whooshing wind build and blow his hair into his eyes.

Noah took a deep breath. He was ready to chase the wind.

BUS STOP

He followed the wind as it whistled down his street,

blustering around buses and bicycles and whipping wrappers from the gutter.

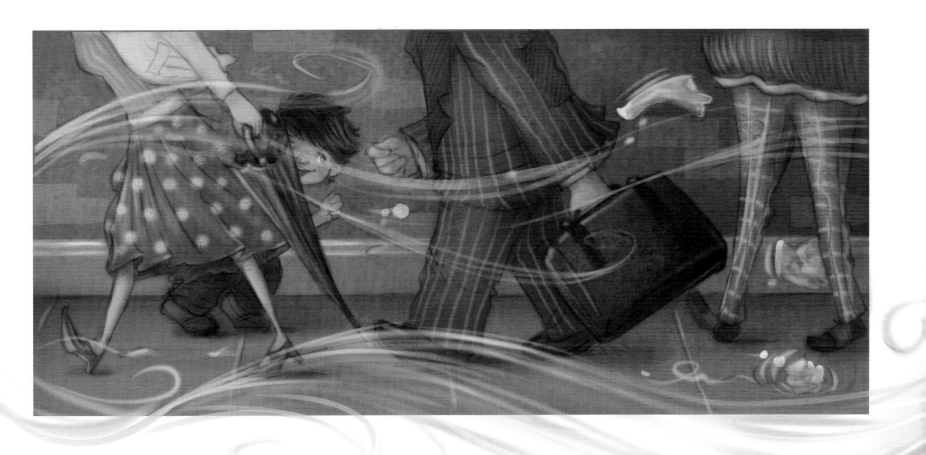

He chased the wind as it glided over fountains, under bridges, and between people on the sidewalk.

He raced the wind as it picked up speed, building with the breeze from the beach and the heat from the highway, growing into a gale that lifted Noah off his feet.

Each stream of air

became a different color,

and Noah was lifted

high above the clouds.

He floated on a blue billowing breeze as the winds whirled and twirled around him in a never-ending ribbon of rainbow.

The wind never stopped moving for a second.

Until eventually, slowly, the blue breeze sank to the ground and Noah could feel the familiar grass underneath his feet. With a brush of Noah's cheek for good-bye, the wind was gone.

Noah sat still until the sun sank below the tops of the trees and his mother called him in for dinner.

"Where have you been?" she asked.

Noah gave her one of his most loving smiles
and said, "I know where the wind goes."

A Note from the Author

Noah sees the world in a unique and special way. He's sensitive and perceptive, and he asks questions many people—both children and adults—never consider. When he can't find the answers to his questions, "it hurts his head and his heart."

Children who see the world differently, whose perceptions are unique, sometimes struggle. It's the job of the grown-ups who care for and teach children to help them feel good about themselves for who they are. All children can learn to understand that being different is okay.

In *Noah Chases the Wind*, my hope is that children who experience the world in a unique way—including children with sensory processing challenges and children on the autism spectrum—will recognize a part of themselves in Noah.

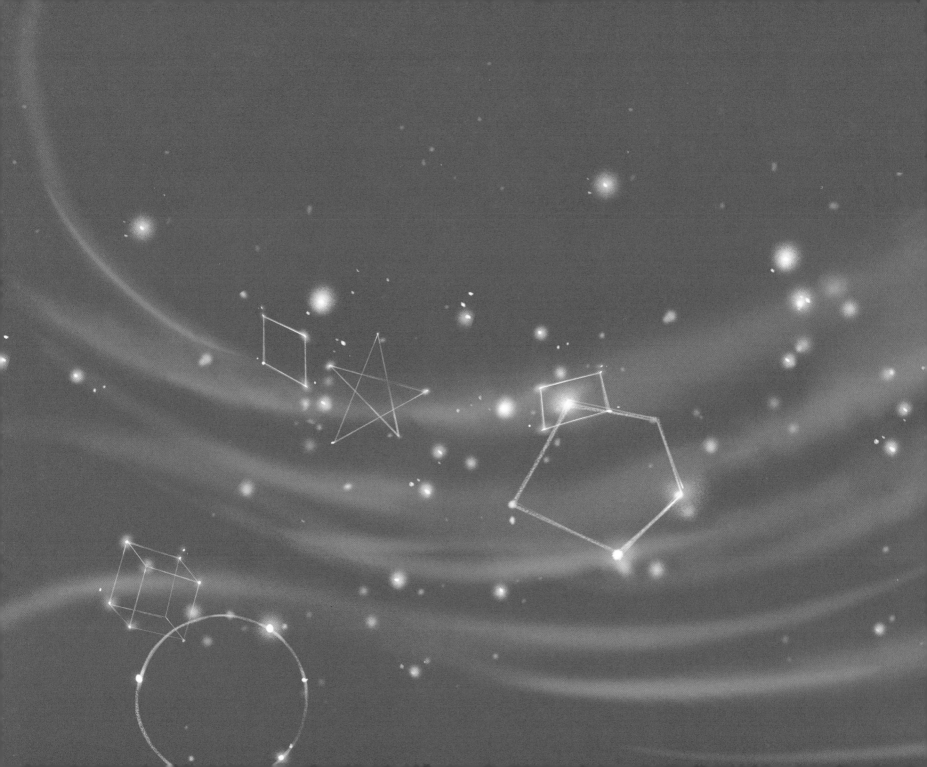